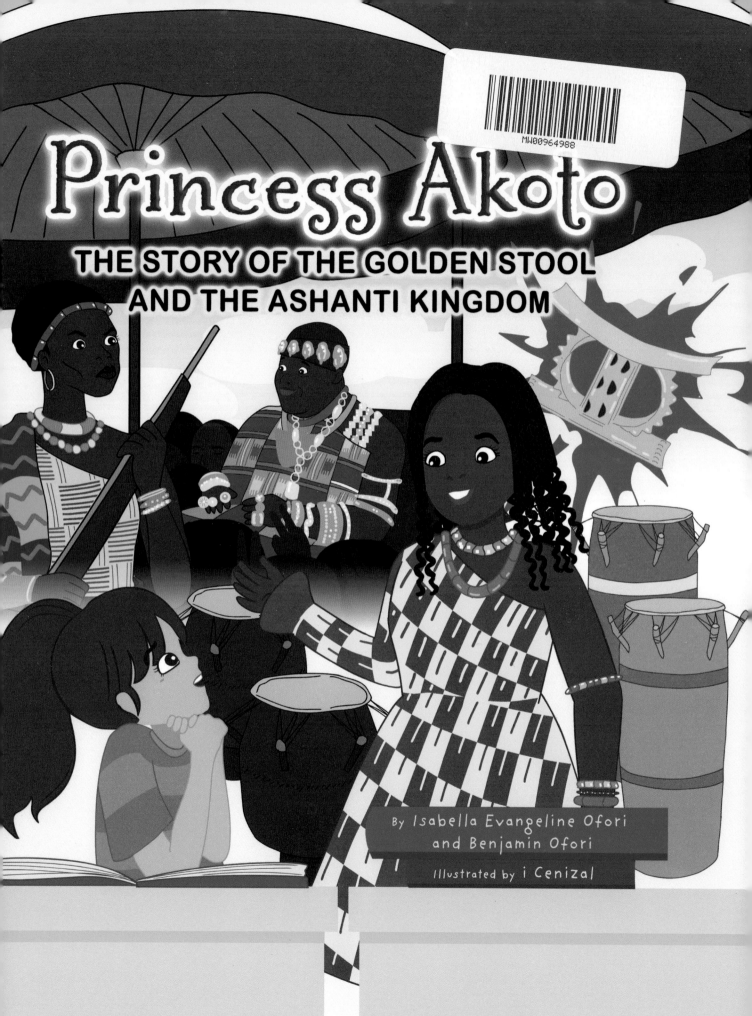

Princess Akoto

THE STORY OF THE GOLDEN STOOL AND THE ASHANTI KINGDOM

By Isabella Evangeline Ofori
and Benjamin Ofori

Illustrated by i Cenizal

MW00964988

Princess Akoto

Copyright © 2020 by Isabella Evangeline Ofori & Benjamin Ofori

All rights reserved. No part of this publication may be reproduced, distributed, or transmitted in any form or by any means, including photocopying, recording, or other electronic or mechanical methods, without the prior written permission of the author, except in the case of brief quotations embodied in critical reviews and certain other non-commercial uses permitted by copyright law.

Tellwell Talent
www.tellwell.ca

ISBN
978-0-2288-3699-5 (Hardcover)
978-0-2288-3698-8 (Paperback)
978-0-2288-4567-6 (eBook)

ACKNOWLEDGEMENTS

With deepest love and appreciation, I dedicate this book to my parents, Mr. Benjamin Ofori and Mrs. Afia Mensah-Ofori.

Their love, support, and encouragement have inspired me to learn more about my roots in Ghana.

As a great-grandchild of the late Nana Boamah Kwabi II, Omanhene (Traditional Chief) of Beposo (Mampong), Ashanti Region of Ghana, the opportunity to put together a historical story about the Ashanti Kingdom for children around the world has been a proud moment and an honour.

I hope this book inspires and encourages readers to learn more about the people of the Ashanti Kingdom in Ghana.

Lastly, a bit shout out to my auntie, Amma Dobere Mensah; cousins, Micah Mensah, Joshua Mensah, Kwame Okuru Mensah, Jnr. Bless Nana Yaw Dobere Mensah and entire Mensah and Ofori families in the United Kingdom, Ghana, and Italy, and other parts of the world.

Zoe was playing alone in the school playground when she noticed that the new girl who joined her class was sitting by herself in the classroom. Zoe ran towards her in the classroom with a big smile, "Good morning!" she said.

"Good morning," replied Princess Akoto with a smile. She was glad to have a friend to play with.

"Your dress is beautiful, very colourful!" Zoe said. She paused to admire at the dress again and then said, "I am Zoe, what's your name?"

"My name is Princess Akoto. I started school this week."

"That is a beautiful name. Is your name from Africa?" asked Zoe.

"Yes, my name comes from Ghana in West Africa. Thank you," replied Princess Akoto.

"You are welcome. Do you like it here?" Zoe asked.

"Yes, I like it, thank you. I also like the teacher; she is very nice," Princess Akoto said with a smile.

"Mrs. Perdue is always nice." Said Zoe.

Princess Akoto moved closer to Zoe and whispered, "I want to tell you a story about my people in Africa."

Zoe chuckled, "Okay, Princess Akoto, go ahead."

After taking a deep breath, Princess Akoto began her story: "I come from a powerful tribe of the Akan group called Ashanti (Asante) in Ghana, West Africa. The Ashanti people have a King. The people of Ashanti are rich, and they have lots of gold."

"Really? so, if I go there, can I find gold?" Zoe asked.

"Yes, yes, you can, many people from around the world go there to buy gold," said Princess Akoto.

"The Ashantis have a stool that is made of gold." Princess Akoto continued.

"Really?" Zoe asked, puzzled.

"My father told me that the Ashanti people believe the Golden Stool was commanded from Heavens by their High Priest called Okomfo Anokye."

"Did it fall from the skies?" Zoe asked, amazed.

"I have no idea." Princess Akoto said.

"Okomfo Anokye, the High Priest, used the Golden Stool as a symbol of unity to bring all the divided tribes of the Ashanti people together," Princess Akoto described.

"The Ashanti people were great warriors."

"Wow!" exclaimed Zoe.

"Yes, they were. The Ashanti people fought so many wars. They even fought with the British a long time ago, when they wanted to take away their Golden Stool to Britain, but the Ashanti people resisted."

"How did that go?" Zoe asked.

"Yaa Asantewaa, the Ashanti Queen Mother, hid the golden stool in a thick forest and gave the British a fake one."

"Very, very smart!" Zoe clapped in excitement.

"Yes. After four battles, with the British suffering multiple defeats, The British finally defeated the Ashanti people."

"They took the Ashanti King, Prempeh I, and the Queen Mother, Yaa Asantewaa, into exile in another country called the Seychelles Island."

"I guess the people were very sad after the British took away their King and Queen Mother," said Zoe.

"Yes, they were." Princess Akoto replied and then added, "In 1921, the Queen Mother died in Seychelles Island."

"Oh, that was sad, did they kill her?" asked Zoe.

"No, she died from natural causes." Princess Akoto said.

She then smiled as she added, "And in 1924, the British brought back the King of the Ashanti people from Seychelles Island. The Ashanti people were delighted that the King had finally returned."

"Yaaaaay!" Zoe laughed.

"So, do you have any festivals?" asked Zoe

"Of course, we do!" Princess Akoto said, "The Ashanti Kingdom celebrates lots of festivals. Some of the festivals are Akwasidae, Awukudae, and Ashanti Yam festivals."

Princess Akoto clapped joyfully as she talked about the festival in Ghana, "During festivals, the Ashanti people wear colourful dresses and beat drums and other musical instruments, like The Seperewa, a stringed harp-lute, Fontomfrom, and Atunpan drums."

"Is there a special dress for the festival?" Zoe asked.

"The Ashanti people sometimes wear Kente Cloth during festivals," said Princess Akoto. "Kente cloth is a typical costume of the Ashanti people."

"Is that like a Halloween costume?" Zoe asked.

"No, Kente is a specially woven cloth made into dresses from colourful fabrics."

"During festivals, the Ashanti people sometimes carry the King in a palanquin." Princess Akoto said. "The King's servants hold a large umbrella as a shade for the King."

"They may be very, very tired," said Zoe.

"Normally, a little girl sits in the palanquin in front of the King," Princess Akoto said.

"Is the little girl the King's daughter?" asked Zoe.

"Not always," replied Princess Akoto. "So many people come to the street to watch the King's procession."

"The King greets the crowd and sometimes dances to the admiration of the people." Princess Akoto explained.

"I would like to sit in front of the King one day," said Zoe.

"Me too," Princess Akoto said, smiling.

SCIENCE

MATH

"Do you know that the Ashanti people are still famous, powerful, and prosperous?" Princess Akoto said.

"I would like to go there one day, yes, I would surely do!" Said Zoe.

"Great, maybe we can go together one day so that I can show you around." Princess Akoto replied, closing her eyes and imagining travelling with Zoe to Ghana.

End

Isabella Evangeline Ofori is a student at Bishop David Motiuk Catholic Elementary/Junior High School in Edmonton, Alberta, Canada. Isabella was born in 2011 in London, United Kingdom. Isabella has ancestral roots in the Ashanti Region of Ghana, West Africa. Isabella is a great-grandchild of the late Nana Boamah Kwabi II, Omanhene (Traditional Chief) of Beposo (Mampong), Ashanti Region of Ghana. Isabella moved to Edmonton, Alberta, Canada in 2012 with her parents, Benjamin Ofori and Mrs. Afia Mensah-Ofori. Isabella loves reading, writing, music and dancing, and modelling in traditional African outfits.